Dear Parent:
Your child's love of reading starts here!

Every child learns to read in a different way and at his or her own speed. Some go back and forth between reading levels and read favorite books again and again. Others read through each level in order. You can help your young reader improve and become more confident by encouraging his or her own interests and abilities. From books your child reads with you to the first books he or she reads alone, there are I Can Read Books for every stage of reading:

SHARED READING
Basic language, word repetition, and whimsical illustrations, ideal for sharing with your emergent reader

BEGINNING READING
Short sentences, familiar words, and simple concepts for children eager to read on their own

READING WITH HELP
Engaging stories, longer sentences, and language play for developing readers

READING ALONE
Complex plots, challenging vocabulary, and high-interest topics for the independent reader

ADVANCED READING
Short paragraphs, chapters, and exciting themes for the perfect bridge to chapter books

I Can Read Books have introduced children to the joy of reading since 1957. Featuring award-winning authors and illustrators and a fabulous cast of beloved characters, I Can Read Books set the standard for beginning readers.

A lifetime of discovery begins with the magical words "I Can Read!"

Visit www.icanread.com for information
on enriching your child's reading experience.

I Can Read Book® is a trademark of HarperCollins Publishers.

Library of Congress cataloging card number: 2009939630
ISBN 978-0-06-185391-3 (trade bdg.)—ISBN 978-0-06-185389-0 (pbk.)

11   12   13   14   15   SCP   10   9   8   7   6   5   ❖   First Edition

I Can Read!

Marley

AND THE RUNAWAY PUMPKIN

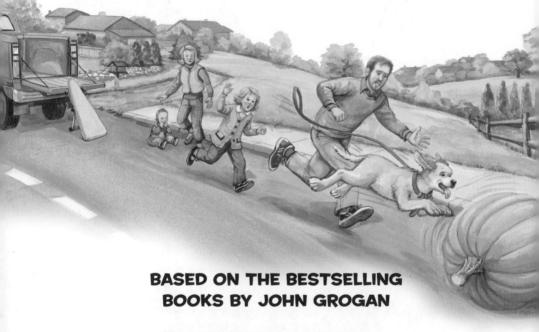

**BASED ON THE BESTSELLING
BOOKS BY JOHN GROGAN**

COVER ART BY RICHARD COWDREY

TEXT BY SUSAN HILL

**INTERIOR ILLUSTRATIONS BY
LYDIA HALVERSON**

HARPER
An Imprint of HarperCollinsPublishers

4

Late one day in fall,

Daddy, Cassie, and Baby Louie

went out to the garden

to look at their pumpkin.

All summer and fall,

the family tended the pumpkin.

They gave it food and water,

sun and shade,

and plenty of room to grow.

All summer and fall,

they kept their big puppy, Marley,

out of the garden.

Now the pumpkin was round.

It was orange.

And it was very, very big.

"Will it win a prize?"

Cassie asked.

Daddy nodded proudly.

"We might even win a blue ribbon,"

he said.

"But first, we have to get

the pumpkin to the fair."

The next day,

Daddy snipped the pumpkin

from the vine.

Mommy helped Daddy roll the pumpkin

to the truck.

Marley batted at the pumpkin.

"That's not a ball, Marley,"

said Mommy.

"That's our blue-ribbon pumpkin!"

Daddy tied Marley up.

"Sorry, Marley," he said,

"but we can't let you mess up

our blue-ribbon pumpkin."

Then Daddy and Mommy tried
to lift the pumpkin onto the truck.
"It's too big to lift," said Mommy.
"What will we do?" asked Cassie.

Daddy went inside and came back
with the ironing board.

"This can be a ramp," he said.

Cassie helped Mommy and Daddy
roll the pumpkin up the ramp.

14

At last, the pumpkin was ready
to go to the fair.

Everybody got behind the pumpkin
so Mommy could take a picture.

"Say blue ribbon!" said Mommy.

Marley wanted to be in the picture.

He tugged at his leash.

Marley broke free

and ran toward the truck.

"No, Marley!" cried Mommy.

Marley made a giant leap,
and landed right on top of
the pumpkin.

The pumpkin rolled out
from under Marley.

The pumpkin rolled out of the truck
and down the ramp,
and then it kept on rolling.

Marley ran after the pumpkin.

Daddy ran after Marley.

Cassie ran after Daddy,

and Baby Louie sat down and cried.

The pumpkin crashed
into the trash cans,
but it didn't slow down.

It bounced onto a scooter,

but it didn't slow down.

Then the pumpkin rolled up
behind the mailman.

"Look out for the pumpkin!"

yelled Cassie.

The mailman jumped out of the way.

"I almost lost my letters,"

said the mailman.

"Look out for Marley!"

yelled Daddy.

But it was too late.

Marley ran into the mailman.

Down went the mailman.

Over went Marley.

Crash went the pumpkin

at the bottom of the hill.

"This is awful," said Cassie.

Mommy gave her a hug.

"When life gives you lemons,

make lemonade," she said.

"And when life gives you

a smashed pumpkin, make pie."

Back at home,

Cassie helped Mommy and Daddy

bake pie.

Lots and lots of pie.

The pie was so good
it won first prize at the fair.

"It was a blue-ribbon pumpkin after all," Cassie said.

And best of all,

there was plenty of pie to share.